SEASONS
OF HER
HEART

SEASONS
OF HER
HEART

A Romantic Novelette

Georgia Jensen Blosil

poetic•arts

www.poetic-arts.com

ISBN: 0-9713601-0-3

Publisher:
poetic•arts
2715 Foothill Drive
Provo, Utah 84604
www.poetic-arts.com

Cover and Book Design:
Paul Shiramizu
Salt Lake City, Utah

Printed in the United States of America

MC Printing
Provo, Utah 84606

ACKNOWLEDGEMENTS

I wish to thank:

My daughter, Kathy...
for the fun of sharing with her
the unfolding of this story, and for
her valued critique of the manuscript.

Paul Shiramizu...
for his exquisite graphic design.

My editor, Stevens Anderson...
for his exceptional guidance,
and his encouragement to publish.

My many friends...
whose enthusiasm for this story
has led to its publication.

My intent was to write a short romantic poem.
As I proceeded, Part One of this novelette
entered my mind instead.

From that time forward
I became a scribe for the story
of a lovely young woman, coming of age,
who suddenly falls in love with a stranger.
I enjoyed being an audience
to the unfolding of her guarded secret,
as she told it to me.

Then she grew older and had more of her story to tell:
She is now a grown woman,
whose heart is ever central to the sentiments
and ambitions of more than one man.
The unexpected and mysterious events
surrounding her life are found in Part Two.

She does not tell us clearly
where and when her story takes place—
only that it is in the distant past.
The intimate and impassioned relationships
of the people involved
are what matter most to her.

PART ONE

The Choice

Chapter One

Down the beckoning hillside,
running fast and free,
I tripped and fell, rolled and rolled
as pebbles skinned my knees.
Sudden bubbling laughter
I did not try to hide,
filled the sunlit meadow air
and banished all my pride.

I lay within a flower patch
to calm my heaving sighs.
Still thinking I was all alone,
I lifted up my eyes.
A tall, imposing figure
that swallowed up the sun,
quickly bent beside me
and made the shadows run.

The grin that stretched a handsome face,
coming much too near,
melted in a gentle voice
that blushed my cheeks and ears.
Deep and resonating tones
asking for my name
made my heart beat wildly—
and I thought to run again.

I raised upon my elbows;
then felt two wide, warm hands
lift me from the brittle grass,
helping me to stand.
I brushed my dusty, tousled hair
and straightened out my skirt.
He watched my every move with flair,
and then began to flirt.

Gently he chided me
for running down the hill,
dressed in skirts and petticoats,
without a thread of skill.
Trying hard to hide my grin,
I turned to walk alone.
His steady footsteps followed
on the pathway to my home.

When I reached the garden gate
I cast a nervous glance,
and stepped within the white-washed fence,
not giving him a chance
to know how much I wondered
how he found me there,
lying in the flower patch—
and why he seemed to care.

I paused within my doorway,
deciding I must ask
(a natural thing to do,
yet embarrassed by the task).
I turned to look behind me;
the sun was hot and bright.
I cupped my hands above my brow;
no one was in sight!

Hurrying to the pathway,
down to the meadow's rim,
turning round and round I searched
to find a glimpse of him.
Then all at once like magic,
in the distance I could see
he sat upon the flower patch
as if to think of me.

A bird-song broke the binding spell.
I raised my eyes to look
up in the tree tops, as they swayed
above the meadow brook.
I gazed back down the hillside—
it did not seem that long—
yet, as magically as he had appeared,
he magically was gone.

Ambling to the garden gate,
my pace now sad and slow,
I pondered what I thought I saw,
and would I ever know
who was the handsome stranger?
Everything it seemed—
his face, his smile, his voice, his hands—
a captivating dream!

Chapter Two

In the village marketplace
I stopped to buy some plums.
A month had passed, and I had thought
that all my dreams were done.
Yet, there among the apple carts
I saw his strident pace
hurry him with firm, long steps—
until he saw my face.

He stopped and stared; I stood erect,
frozen with delight.
I held my breath and gave a smile
that meant to be polite.
He tipped his hat and walked away;
then with a second thought
turned around, approached my side
to ask what I had bought.

"Plums," I said, and offered one
to mask my great surprise.
We both began to laugh, and then
something caught his eyes.
A voice behind me called his name,
"Robert, over here!
I looked for you around the square"—
the words came bright and clear.

Then I beheld a silken sleeve
that wrapped a slender arm,
reach beside my shoulder
with a studied, graceful form.
Her perfume sweetly blended
with the fragrance of the fruit,
as a young and lovely woman
gladly ended her pursuit.

She rushed to Robert's side,
and with a proud, possessive pose
she turned to look upon me
and tilted up her nose.
Her hat was broadly brimmed
with purple ribbons at the crown.
Her face was pink and polished,
her eyes were chocolate brown.

Robert seemed to relish
her fond, familiar embrace.
He was visibly amused to see
the shock upon my face.
Taking her by the hand,
he gently spoke her name:
"Helene," he said, "I must admit
I am the one to blame.

I sauntered through the marketplace
while you were in a shop.
Thinking you would be a while
I never thought to stop,
until I saw this maiden,
whom I have met before.
I do not recall her name."
Then he looked at me once more.

"My name is Ruth," I offered
with modesty of tone.
"If you will please excuse me,
I must be getting home."
Helene's reply was curt and cold.
She pulled on Robert's hand.
"We must also go," she affirmed.
"Meeting you was grand."

Her quick and condescending words
were meant to let me know
her station was above my own,
and she must never show
an interest in a country maid
who had no social worth.
I knew she would feel differently
if she could know the truth.

I glanced again at Robert
who began a manly bow.
Upon his solemn face I saw
a frown upon his brow.
I gave a graceful curtsy;
then with a stately air,
I turned, and whirled my cotton skirts,
pretending not to care

that I was clearly out of place
in Robert's company.
Helene was much too elegant,
one could clearly see
her beauty caught attention
throughout the market square.
Everything about her
eclipsed my presence there.

I wandered somewhat aimlessly
through the village streets
to hide myself among the crowds,
hoping not to meet
another new acquaintance
who would surely see the tears.
They swelled within my eyes,
increasing all my fears

of losing anonymity
I intended to maintain.
I needed precious time alone
before I must again
return from simple country life,
the peaceful reverie,
and the flower-covered meadow
that meant so much to me.

When I reached my cottage door
rain began to fall.
Gathering clouds hung down low,
darkening the hall
that led me to the parlor
where my books were lying still.
Like such good friends they greeted me
and soothed the autumn chill.

Summer quickly came and went.
The trees in leafless form
were etched against the greying sky.
A fierce, forbidding storm
sang above the rooftop.
I shivered with the sound.
Whirling leaves filled the air
and raced across the ground.

I lit a candle, pulled the shades,
and lay upon my bed.
Thoughts of Robert filled my mind.
The words he briefly said
haunted me with questions,
as the candle flickered low
and cast a magic spell that made
the shadows ebb and flow.

I knew I had been foolish
to let another man
distract me from commitments
I must try to understand.
Still, I yearned for his attentions,
despite my brief alarm,
remembering how he lifted me
in his strong, protective arms.

I knew nothing of his life,
nor from whence he came.
Trying to forget him
would ever be in vain.
"Robert, Robert, who are you?
Why did you find me there
in the flowered meadow,
then in the market square?"

Chapter Three

Morning sunshine bathed the frost
that sparkled on the grass.
My coach stood at the garden gate.
How quickly time had passed
from summer's warmth to fall's embrace!
Now winter at the door
greeted me with stinging winds
that made the meadow roar.

Riding past the village,
in the distance I could see
the market square was empty,
like the emptiness in me.
As the horses pulled me onward,
their quick and steady trot
lulled my aching heart to sleep,
until the coach did stop

beside a stream of water
to give the horses drink.
The pause upon the roadside
awakened me to think
of the dinners and the dances
that soon would fill my home.
I knew among the many guests
I still would feel alone.

"Father walking by my side,
and mother, full of glee,
will lead me to their ballroom
to present the 'bride to be.'
Paul will then step forward,
take me by the hand,
then guide me in a spinning waltz.
The other guests will stand

with rapt attention while we twirl,
waiting for their turn.
My gracious manners, well observed,
will never let them learn—
somewhere in the countryside
there is another man
who made my heart beat faster
than any other can.

Paul will be so eager
to set the wedding date.
I have tried in every way
to make our families wait.
They never understood me;
they thought I should comply
with plans they made, and as a girl
I promised them to try.

While in my youth and innocence,
Paul was a fine young lad
who made me laugh and gave me gifts
I never would have had.
Through every year as I grew up
my promise did hold true.
In time all my feelings changed
to something very new."

The coachman snapped the horses' reigns;
the carriage, with a lurch,
traveled down a widening road
and passed a stately church.
By then my thoughts had shifted
from the distant past, to present fears.
"How could I break a promise
I had kept for all those years?

Could I explain that marriage
was a childhood fantasy?
Paul was just a cherished friend
who made my future seem to be
so comfortable and natural,
predictable, secure.
Yet, there are deep emotions
mere friendship cannot stir.

Still, it would be improper.
It would be so cruel.
Marriage plans like ours were made
within strict social rules.
Undoubtedly in time,
and with children in my life,
Paul could make me happy
and content to be his wife."

My logic helped console me
with compensatory pride.
"I can be quite noble
as a dedicated bride—
attending social gatherings
with those who wish me well,
and not let on my struggles
with a truth I cannot not tell."

The coach was slowing down,
as the sun began to set.
In just a few more miles I knew
my dreams I must forget—
except a handsome stranger
with just his given name.
"Robert, now I know that we
must never meet again."

Chapter Four

Christmas bells began to peal
resounding everywhere.
My heart was cheered with laughter
and excitement in the air.
Far and wide the owners
of each elegant estate
take a turn inviting friends
to come and celebrate.

Decorations, Christmas trees
elegant and tall,
bring rapt anticipation
for the festive Christmas balls—
where ladies in their finest gowns
adorn each crowded room
with their satins, silks and laces,
and costly French perfumes.

The mothers of the debutantes
all keep a watchful eye
to see where all the young men are,
hoping each will try
to meet their lovely daughters
and ask them for a dance,
which could be the welcome onset
of a lasting new romance.

I dutifully attended
each party of the year.
I had reached the proper age
when debutantes appear
to take their social places.
It was widely known to all
that promises were made—
and I belonged to Paul.

It didn't seem to matter
that all the young men knew.
At every social gathering,
when Paul was out of view,
each bachelor in his clever way,
each way that he could find,
would take his turn pursuing me
to try and change my mind.

Paul would always notice,
everywhere I went,
men would flock to flirt with me.
It wasn't my intent
to invite their bold attentions.
Paul could never hide
how it made him jealous,
yet it always piqued his pride.

The time had come for our estate
to host a Christmas ball.
Delaying the announcement
that I would marry Paul,
my father and my mother,
though feeling some chagrin,
agreed to let me wait once more—
perhaps until the spring.

Our dining hall was filled with food.
Candles everywhere
guided guests from room to room
to see who might be there.
Some would bring important friends
who came from distant lands
to meet the local gentry,
and who made each party grand.

Part way through the evening,
after dancing many times,
I gave my most coquettish bow,
then quickly left the lines
of the ladies and the gentlemen
who stood across the floor—
all waiting for the music
to fill the room once more.

I left the bustling ballroom
to seek out some repose,
and to pat the perspiration
that was glistening on my nose.
My well coiffed hair was falling
from the combs that held it high.
Not wanting to be noticed,
I knew that I should try

to slip up to my bedroom,
where I would have the time
to recover my appearance.
As I began to climb
the graceful, winding staircase
within our spacious entrance,
I heard my father's voice,
as he welcomed in the presence

of new and unexpected guests.
My mother, close behind,
rushed across the marble floor.
Always warm and kind,
and with her effervescent charm
she spoke alarming words:
"What a lovely, sweet surprise!
Everyone had heard

that you, Helene, had traveled home.
And, Robert, I had thought
that with your business now completed
you would not care to stop
for Christmas celebrations here
before you left again.
It is so nice to see you;
I am so very glad you came."

Chapter Five

My mind was stunned, my head felt faint.
I reeled with disbelief.
For the moment no one saw me,
which engendered some relief.
"Was this the couple Mother met
and seemed so glad to know?"
I paid it no attention,
for so many people go

to the parties and the ladies' teas
presented every week.
My mother never gave the names
whenever she would speak
of those who most impressed her.
And I made no requests—
who they were and what they said
barely kept my interest.

Helene strutted in the entry,
then pompously complied
with Mother, chattering with delight,
who kept her occupied.
As they moved to an adjoining room
I was relieved to see—
I must have gone unnoticed,
for neither one looked up at me.

And then it happened! Robert paused
and lifted his grey-blue eyes.
He stood transfixed; moments passed,
as then I realized
he saw me on the staircase.
My dress was crimson red.
The skirts were full, the bodice tight.
Candles lit my head.

The moments seemed to hold us
like a warm and strong embrace.
I could not move while looking down
at Robert's handsome face.
I heard my father's happy voice
invite me to descend
to meet the new arriving guests.
I knew I must pretend

to make a first acquaintance
with Robert. Would he guess?
Was I the same young maiden
in the simple country dress
who fell among the flowers—
and in a crowded market square
left him so abruptly
because Helene was also there?

As I was drawing close to him,
he could not shift his gaze.
His wondering eyes were held in mine.
All else seemed in a haze.
When I stood beside my father,
Robert carefully perused
my face, my hair, my crimson dress,
appearing most bemused.

Then Father spoke convincing words:
"Please meet my daughter, Ruth."
With such an introduction,
surely Robert knew the truth.
With a bow, he cast that smile
I cherished in my dreams.
Far away I heard Paul's voice,
"Ruth, where have you been?"

It broke the spell. I felt again
my body start to sway.
Startled by reality,
I wished to run away.
I tried to look delighted;
I feared that I looked white.
What had been a festive ball
had become a shocking night.

Again my father took control.
With an eager voice,
he invited Paul to where we stood,
giving him no choice
but to face the man whose presence there
confirmed my hidden pain—
I never would forget him!
He stirred my heart again

with feelings warm and thrilling;
yet they also made me sad.
Such compelling feelings
were those I should have had
to make a promise to a man
that I would be his bride.
The guilt returned with anger,
as Paul, now at my side,

placed an arm around my waist,
drawing me quite near—
a gesture to another man,
making it quite clear
that I was more than just his friend.
The message that he sent
was pointed and defensive.
Robert knew just what it meant.

They spoke in brief, politely.
Then Robert turned to me.
"I thought that we had met before,
but now we must agree,
I was mistaken." With a nod,
he promptly strode away.
Paul remarked, "How very odd!
Was that all he could say?

Ruth, it is time you danced with me,
for it is getting late."
He drew me to the ballroom.
I could not hesitate,
although my hair had fallen—
my face crestfallen too.
"What must Robert think of me?
What am I to do?"

My thoughts were racing with despair.
Somehow I must endure.
Across the room I spied Helene;
she was the perfect cure
for all my thoughts of self-defeat.
I stiffened with resolve.
Before the festive night would end,
I planned to get involved

with all the ladies' gossip,
and find out who she was;
then introduce myself to her,
and hope to give her cause
for feeling quite embarrassed—
as she once embarrassed me
in the village market.
I wanted her to see

that I could be quite haughty,
and I could act quite proud,
with my towering social status,
and among the lustrous crowd
of those esteemed and honored guests
who clamored for the chance
to meet my charming parents
at their annual Christmas Dance.

By now my curls were settling
on my shoulders free and full,
just above my slender back—
breaking fashion rules—
appearing like a gypsy.
This pleased the gawking men
who crowded all around me
before the dance began.

The musicians had assembled;
music filled the air.
People from around the floor
vacated every chair.
As the dancers came together,
the men by me dispersed;
for Paul complained that I was meant
to waltz with him at first.

When they began to move away
I noticed in a glance,
Robert had been watching
with an agitated stance.
"Does he think that I am brazen
and just a heartless flirt?"
Somehow it gave me pleasure
to imagine he was hurt.

"What nonsense! What a fool I am
to play this childish game
with my turbulent emotions.
What do I hope to gain?"
Paul took me in his arms
and we waltzed with style and grace.
As we withdrew from Robert,
I no longer saw his face.

I must admit, my dress, my hair,
my unbridled attitude
caught everyone's attention,
for my actions did intrude
upon the other couples.
Paul, taking me aside,
cautioned me with earnest words.
By then he did not hide

his possessive disposition.
I would not yield at all.
This was a night I refused to care
if I offended Paul.
Incensed by his reprimands,
I almost caused a scene.
But I needed to be proper,
or else it would demean

my parents, who so much desired
to please their honored guests.
The waltz was drawing to a close;
the dancers stopped to rest.
During the musicians' pause
I sensed a man's advance.
I heard a voice behind me say,
"I trust we have this dance."

Paul was startled—yet the words
quieted his defense.
I felt a wide, warm hand in mine,
increasing the suspense
that it was Robert's voice I heard.
I turned my eyes to see.
He took me in his arms and said,
"This waltz belongs to me."

When the music started,
in Robert's strong embrace,
knowing how he smiled
I dared not look upon his face.
I could not breathe; I could not speak.
"How can this all be true—
held again by Robert's arms,
my thoughts provoked anew

to break a long-held promise
I meant to be sincere?"
Suddenly I saw Helene
and felt a rush of tears—
lingering tears I had fought to hide
within the market square—
bewildering tears I held inside
and carried everywhere.

I stumbled as I lost my step;
then Robert held me tight.
I leaned my head upon his chest
and prayed that just this night
I might release my feelings.
And yet, I pushed away.
Deep into his grey-blue eyes,
I gazed as if to say,

"This is wrong; I lost my head.
Don't tempt my heart again."
Robert's marked confusion
added to my pain.
Before we could begin to speak,
Paul was at my side.
With no restraint, he boasted,
"Ruth is soon to be my bride."

Unruffled, Robert cocked his head.
(He took the message as a threat.)
"I beg your pardon, Sir," he said,
"but let us not forget
that dancing with the daughter
of a gentleman and host
is a simple act of courtesy
at the very most."

Robert confidently stood his ground,
with no intent to move away.
By then Helene had joined us,
and she went on to say,
"Robert, introduce me, please."
With her radiant charm,
she beamed at Paul, ignoring me,
and cuddled Robert's arm.

Robert knowingly turned to Paul,
and instead to him replied:
"We must both be going now.
So nice to meet your bride."
Then he glanced at me with solemn eyes.
Helene was unaware
that I was Ruth, the country maid;
by then I did not care.

Paul just stared without a word.
And I, with speechless shame,
watched Robert and Helene retreat.
I had myself to blame
for inciting Paul to be so rude,
for my flirtatious acts.
I had been trained how one behaves
with modesty and tact.

Chapter Six

When I retired, my nerves so taut,
the creaking in the room
kept me awake with restless thought—
morning came too soon.
The glowing dawn aroused within me
questions strange and new.
The smile Helene had cast at Paul
demanded my review.

I pondered how she beckoned him
with well rehearsed allure.
The intentions in her eyes were clear.
Then to be quite sure,
as she moved across the dance floor
with an undulating stroll,
she turned and beamed at Paul once more.
I fought so to control

my mix of strong emotions.
As she left the room,
I snapped at Paul, reminding him
he was to be my groom!
This shocked us both; Paul was pleased.
The twinkle in his eyes
swelled my flustered attitude.
Then to his surprise,

I stormed across the entry hall
and darted up the stairs.
Tears began to bathe my face
confusing all my cares
for Robert and Helene and Paul—
each one tormented me!
I slammed my bedroom door;
then through the window I could see

that Robert and Helene were gone.
I feared that they might know
how rudely I had scolded Paul
and let my anger show.
Exhausted by the whole ordeal,
I slumped upon a chair
before my dresser mirror.
I then began to stare

at my hair—in total disarray;
my cheeks were wet and flushed.
I tore the hem of my ball gown
when up the stairs I rushed
to end the long and frightful night,
and drown myself in sleep.
Perhaps by morning I could bear
the secrets I must keep.

Chapter Seven

My mother stood beside our coach
with great anticipation,
calling me to hurry
and fulfill my obligation
to condescend and go with her
to a ladies' tea.
She seemed to think the curious guests
would all be missing me

if I failed to join the mothers
and their daughters for the chance
to reminisce and gossip
about our prestigious Christmas dance.
Yes, I was still embarrassed,
regretful, and ashamed
for losing my composure
when Helene and Robert came.

"On Christmas Eve, a gathering—
at our parish hall—
will come to hear a concert choir
before the evening ball.
If they both attend the program,
then I will be discreet,
behaving as a lady should
no matter how we meet."

My introspection ended
when our coach reeled to a stop
before the home of neighboring friends,
abruptly ending all my thoughts
of what I did and how I felt.
I knew I must prepare
for the ladies' conversations
and the comments they would share.

After I was welcomed
by the hostess at her door,
I hurried to the dining room,
deciding to explore
the thoughts of all the ladies
who were present in our home
when Robert and Helene arrived,
and what they might have known.

"Until the tea comes to an end,
their many observations
I must handle with great caution
to avoid their speculations."
As I approached two chatting ladies,
I overheard the one reply
that Paul was just the man she knew
caught every woman's eye.

"He is so handsome and romantic;
no bachelor can compare.
All the lovely debutantes
are hoping he will dare
to reconsider his intent,
and recognize the truth
that he has captured every heart.
He need not marry Ruth!"

Then the ladies turned their backs
so no one else could hear.
I crept a little closer,
while straining both my ears.
What they started whispering
sounded like a monstrous scheme.
I heard them giggling over something
that sounded like "Helene!"

One said, "She asked a lady,
who is in another room,
to tell her all about a man
she plans to visit soon.
They walked and talked for quite some time
within a private hall.
Everyone observing them
could tell they spoke of Paul!"

By then I knew Helene was there
among my mother's friends.
I wondered what would come of this
if I did not defend
Paul's sterling reputation,
and his promise made to me.
"How could he plan a visit
with a woman such as she?"

The gossip proved distressing.
I could not bear to stay
and see that flirt Helene again.
I found a gracious way
to let the kindly hostess know
I was not feeling well.
I asked that she excuse me,
and find someone to tell

my mother that I had to leave.
I would later send
our coach to come and bring her home
before the tea would end.
The wintry breeze refreshed my mind.
Ice crystals, all aglow,
crunched beneath my footsteps,
as I crossed the dazzling snow.

Brilliant white illumination
swept across the land,
and lit my contemplative mind
to help me understand
that what I had been feeling
for Robert, most of all
were undiscovered feelings
that I also felt for Paul!

Chapter Eight

The Christmas choir had ended.
Steeple bells began to ring.
Carolers assembled,
merrily to sing
within the parish courtyard,
and down the snowy lanes.
Candlelight sparkled bright
through stained-glass window panes.

Coaches lined the roadside,
the horses stood with ease.
Snow fell off the branches
of the heavy-laden trees.
I had not seen Robert—
Helene, no where in sight—
I wondered, "Will they both appear
later in the night?"

The throng of guests arriving
at the elegant estate
chattered with excitement.
None of them could wait
to assemble in a room
where a bounteous table stood,
to drink the warming wassail
and taste the festive food.

I stepped into the ballroom,
for the music had begun.
Some bachelors rushed beside me,
asking who had won
my first dance of the evening.
My distracted mind was filled
with private contemplation.
I remained erect and still.

Across the floor I saw Helene.
Her manifest allure
had captivated Paul
as he made an overture.
He pulled her close; their waltz began.
"Where could Robert be?"
I left the ballroom, making sure
they did not notice me.

All the ladies' gossip,
Paul asking her to dance,
convinced me he had been seduced
into a new romance.
"Helene has been victorious.
Her surreptitious schemes
have turned Paul's fickle head away
from all his youthful dreams!"

I fled within the walls
of a small and darkened room.
Still lost in thought, I leaned beside
a window where the moon
cast soft and silken strands of light
through the fragile lace
of long cascading curtains
that draped the window space.

I was weary of the parties,
and the boring conversations
of the ladies and the gentlemen
seeking adulation
by their repetitious stories
of where everybody went,
and who was there and what they wore
at every grand event!

I yearned again for country life,
for meadow brooks and flowers.
I missed a cottage filled with books
where I could read for hours;
and walk the village pathways,
and shop the village square
for simple foods and artifacts
that the people living there

harvest from their gardens,
and make with their own hands.
At the ending of a peaceful day
there would be no demands
for social obligations,
and the complicated rules
I had to learn and practice
in strict and stuffy schools.

As I stood within the silent room—
content to be alone—
I heard a voice behind me ask,
"May I escort you home?"
"Home?" I said. "It is early."
It was then I turned my head.
A man stood in the doorway
where my searching eyes were led.

I could barely see his form.
The shadows from the wall
darkened his tall figure—
yet I knew the man was Paul.
He moved across the floor;
then stood so I could see
his solemn face and gentle eyes
gazing down at me.

"The ladies and their gossip
and the debutantes are right.
Paul is handsome and romantic.
Why must it be this night
that I finally see him
as a grown and noble man?
When did it happen; where was I?
Now I fully understand

what I have never noticed—
there before my eyes—
Paul is the man I have always loved.
Now I must disguise
my honest feelings for him,
for Helene has won his heart.
It is too late—my thoughtless ways
have ruined every part

of the happiness he gave me,
the promises we made.
His patience and his kindness
can never be repaid."
Paul placed a hand upon my cheek
and lifted up my chin.
He paused for my reaction,
and then began to grin.

"Ruth, you know I love you.
I have for all these years.
When you were just a little girl,
I comforted your tears.
I played your games and answered
all the questions you would ask.
You looked for me to help you
with your every childhood task.

Each time we were together,
alone or in a crowd,
remember how you followed me
whenever I allowed
a most precocious little girl
to deftly spy on me?
No matter where I went
I saw you hiding by a tree

or peeking through the bushes.
I knew you were there.
You couldn't hide your billowy skirts
or the ribbons in your hair.
Now you are a maiden,
and I am a desperate man!
I want you to become my wife.
I promise that you can

follow me forever.
But I want you at my side.
You need not peek at me again,
nor feel that you must hide."
His sweet proposal made me laugh,
and then I had to cry.
With rushing, stammering words I spoke,
as tears spilled from my eyes:

"Dearest Paul, will you forgive me?
I will never hide again.
How very much I love you!
Now quickly, tell me when
I may willingly become your wife
and end my cruel delay?"
Paul drew me in his arms
and warmly kissed my words away.

Chapter Nine

Our parents were ecstatic
to hear the welcome news
that Paul and I would marry,
as soon as they would choose.
We set an early wedding date,
just time enough for plans
that excited both our mothers.
They wanted something grand

to celebrate the blessed event,
inviting all their friends.
The debutantes and bachelors
knew it was the end
of their pursuits of Paul and me.
However, we could tell
how quick they were to eye each other,
as they came to wish us well.

A few days before our wedding
Paul received a pleasant note.
His mother's aunt would soon arrive—
excitedly she wrote—
to personally bestow a gift
especially for Paul.
He was her favorite nephew,
though she seldom came to call.

When she had seated Paul and me
upon two parlor chairs,
while opening an envelope
that held her own affairs,
she spoke: "My darling nephew,
I have a special charge.
It comes from your dear grandfather—
it is beautiful and large.

In the country is a manor-house,
one of his estates.
He has wanted you to have it,
but preferred to make you wait
to see if you would marry Ruth;
he adored her since a child.
When he visited her parents,
she told of flowers wild

within the country meadows,
chattering with delight
all about the beauty
that she gathered in her sight.
He knew her heart was ever there
among the simple things,
lending comfort to the senses
that only nature brings.

Now, my dear Paul and Ruth,
I hope you will agree
to accept this generous gift,
for it does not come from me."
Breathlessly, I grinned at Paul,
who nodded to his Aunt
an affirmative assurance.
He would surely grant

the wishes of his grandfather,
and bless me with a home
near the meadow fields of flowers
where I could daily roam,
and listen to the bird-songs—
sit beside the meadow brook,
and read for cherished, endless hours
my own beloved books.

That evening in my parent's home,
friends and family filled the rooms
for our engagement party
and to greet the bride and groom.
Amid the celebration,
I reflected on my past
and the memories of my childhood
that now pleasantly would last.

Chapter Ten

Now you may be wondering
what happened to Helene—
and Robert, to my grand surprise,
who walked into my dreams?
Yes, his grey-blue eyes, engaging smile
inspired my maiden heart
with profound romantic feelings
that he alone would start.

Helene is Robert's sister
whom he brought for company
while he was doing business
in our region. It was she
who requested to remain
for our parties of the season.
Robert graciously complied,
for she had avid social reasons.

When the Christmas balls ended,
they shortened up their stay.
Unexpectedly as they appeared,
they quietly slipped away.
No one else need tell me,
nor offer to explain,
why they left without goodbyes,
and will not come again.

I suspect their hastened departure
was for Robert's sake alone.
At our every brief encounter,
in the country and my home,
Robert's fascination for me
was as strong as mine for him.
I could see it in his eyes, his smile—
and felt it deeply from within.

Surely, Robert knew his presence
brought an awakening to me—
within our shared attraction,
he unveiled my eyes to see:
There within my hopes and dreams
Paul was the only man
who could make my heart beat faster
than any other can.

Throughout our country manor,
children's voices sing.
And when the wintry frost has gone,
early in the spring,
we romp within the meadow
and shop the village square.
My happiness is now complete,
for Paul is with me there.

PART TWO

The Gift

Chapter One

I traveled to the seashore,
my children at my side,
to a place we had not been before,
a place where we could hide.
The children climbed the rocks and moss.
It was more than two long years
since we had mourned their father's loss
and spent our bitter tears.

I was content to rest and read
this unfamiliar land,
and watch the waves ascend and weave
through driftwood on the sand.
The children's laughter blended
with the seagulls' beckoning calls.
Such happy moments ended
when my thoughts returned to Paul.

Time it was to shed the black,
the clothes I chose for me.
I knew Paul never would come back.
I needed to be free
from words of pity said and sent,
the never-ending quest
of those who cared, of those who meant
to put my grief to rest.

Perhaps I thought the ocean spray
would wash away the pain,
somehow ease the lonely day,
bringing peace again.
Oh, how I fought the wearying weight
of memories old and stark
that once were sweet and bright; now fate
had turned them sour and dark.

My trust and hope had lingered on,
long after Paul had left.
I did my best, despite the wrong.
His love and his respect
scorned by friends who scathed his name,
denouncing what he did.
I had to brave the stinging shame
that never could be hid.

Paul had to take a journey
many days away from home.
As the trip would be quite lengthy,
he traveled all alone.
His mother's maiden aunt was ill,
she called him to her side
to handle her affairs—until
she failed and later died.

Paul was her favorite nephew,
he would be her only heir.
His love for her was deep and true,
he helped her with great care.
When her estate was put away
and all the work was done,
I knew Paul had no need to stay,
so homeward he would come.

Sometime later I would learn
he must have stopped to rest
in a country village tavern.
His steed—one of the best—
he selected from our stables
on the morning he left home.
It was strong and young and able,
a large and lovely roan.

The horse would not delay him,
and Paul took so much pride
in how his mount could always win
each race with easy stride.
I pondered where the horse might be,
and where it carried Paul
from loving children, home, and me.
I pondered most of all:

They said her beauty made men stare.
Her wide and wandering eyes
saw Paul within the village square—
a wealthy, handsome prize.
She feigned to be a messenger
with urgent, private news:
He must quickly follow her,
not wait and not refuse.

Paul looked upon her earnest face;
then with her gift of guile
she lured him to an unknown place.
Her captivating smile
was known to all the village men
who watched her play that game.
They told the story where and when
Paul was not seen again.

A search was made, weeks went by.
Paul was never found.
Then someone with a careful eye
noticed on the ground,
beside a dusty tavern chair,
a letter meant for me.
How it happened to be there
remains a mystery.

I recognized Paul's signature,
his message, short and firm:
He said he was in love with her,
and he would not return.
So clear to me without delay
the writing was his own,
when last the letter found its way
and journeyed to our home.

Friends had tried to search her name—
a quest I never dared.
It would not lift the bitter blame
that she and Paul both shared.
Somewhere they were together,
such thoughts, cruel company!
And memories last forever.
There were quite enough for me.

Chapter Two

It was time for Jennie's birthday,
time to leave the ocean shore,
and return to home where she could play
with toys and friends once more.
She was turning nine years old,
a most precocious child
with charming manners, I was told:
Merry, modest and mild.

Peter was so much like Paul,
with handsome face and form;
a lad whose fond observers called
"a prince" since he was born.
He was twelve, just old enough
to bear the ridicule
that made his feelings cold and tough.
They were his chosen rule.

The night I walked the moonlit shore
before our journey home,
I wondered what would be in store.
Would I remain alone
locked within this strict and confining
space I occupied?
Was there a place where I could sing,
where tears would not be cried?

As I sat and pondered every choice
Paul and I once planned,
I heard a long-forgotten voice,
and felt a wide, warm hand
touch my shoulder tenderly;
a whisper spoke my name.
I turned my startled eyes to see
a familiar face again.

"Robert, Robert! Could this be?
After all the years—
to find within my reverie,
somehow you appear!
How could you know where I had gone?
This distant, barren land
has sheltered me from everyone."
My thoughts bade me to stand.

Robert's eyes—still grey and blue—
softly searched my face.
He paused; then all at once he drew
me to his strong embrace.
The pounding of the restless sea,
the heavy misty air,
swallowed my discretion while he
held me closely there.

Robert's arms released me from
an all consuming daze.
My momentary dream was done.
The questions that he raised
embarrassed me for yielding to
the touch of his kind hand.
He spoke of Paul and what he knew.
He did not understand

why no one learned where Paul had gone;
surely there were clues.
I told him none were very strong.
All that could be used
were long-since put together
into many vain attempts
to bring resolve. And whether
I would ever be content

to let this mystery lead me
into apathy for Paul,
I needed rest from sympathy.
I needed most of all
to find another life-long plan.
My children must forget
their father's loss—how it began—
to gain their self respect.

I asked Robert how he found me
walking on this moonlit shore.
He replied,"I also love the sea.
I saw you once before
playing with your children
on a most fortuitous day.
I kept my presence hidden,
thought it best to slip away.

However, I could not dismiss
a pressing, strong desire
to speak with you, and not to miss
the moment to inquire
about your general welfare,
and offer—as a friend—
whatever comfort I might share.
Despite the sudden end

of our previous brief acquaintance,
I remember you so well—
how every bachelor took his chance,
within your binding spell,
to compete with all the other men
who hovered at your side
to dance with you. It was then
they kept you occupied.

At the Christmas party I attended
in your parent's home;
their pursuits of you would never end,
never leaving you alone."
His chiding brought us laughter;
the memories were sweet.
I sensed that he was after
another time when we could meet.

He said he had not yet married;
he loved someone long ago.
"Circumstances interfered,
and I could not let her know."
Then he became quite sober—
his silence made me blush.
The time for talk was over.
He paused; then in a rush,

he said that it was getting late,
and I must be getting cold.
May he walk me home to compensate
for being quite so bold
to interrupt my privacy?
He hoped not to offend
the friendship that he felt for me.
I knew I must defend

his tender feelings of remorse,
or thoughts that he was wrong
to share concerns for me. Of course
they properly belonged
within the time and present scheme
of our respective lives.
To me, our new-found friendship seemed
a welcome, grand surprise.

That stunning night the moonlit skies
bathed his towering frame
and reflected from his grey-blue eyes.
My mind was filled again
with memories of the way we met.
My girlhood fascinations
for him I never would forget.
Romantic recollections

started flowing easily
as we walked along the beach.
In silence he would glance at me.
As soon as we had reached
the place where we would have to part,
I quickly let him know
his words had comforted my heart.
Tomorrow I must go

to take my children home again.
At a future time, somehow,
I hoped that he would visit when
his business would allow.
He promised he would do so;
then his fingers touched my face.
It was difficult to see him go,
again he caused my heart to race.

Chapter Three

Arriving late at night
at our quiet country estate,
a window full of candlelight
told me Brent would wait,
until he knew that we were well
and safely home again,
assuring him with tales to tell,
how good our trip had been.

Brent came to give assistance
when he learned that Paul was gone.
Despite my kind resistance,
he insisted he belonged
as an only cousin close to Paul
meant to oversee
Paul's estate—and, most of all,
to guard and care for me.

Brent had not yet married,
so no one need complain
about the time with me he shared.
He also could explain
some details of Paul's travels
I never would have known.
Mysteries were unravelled—
some better left alone.

I stepped into the doorway,
entered the darkened hall.
The children promptly raced away
and then began to call,
"We're home!" with voices full of glee.
Their Nanny was surprised.
She gave them hugs and smiled at me
with fondness in her eyes.

So long she nursed me faithfully,
whenever I was ill
with anguish from cruel memories
that lingered with me still.
Brent was simply overjoyed,
now that we were home.
He could not wait to show the toys
he purchased on his own

to give to little Jennie.
Tomorrow was the day
we would celebrate her birth. For me,
it was hard to say
all the words of gratitude
I had for Brent's kind heart.
I told him he was much too good—
I could not even start!

He reached to draw me near.
(I always would resist.)
His sentiments were clear;
he wanted to be kissed.
And, yet, his fond affections
were uncomfortable for me.
He often shared his expectations:
"One day you will be free

to love again another man."
He wanted me to try.
"I don't know if I ever can,"
was always my reply.
Brent would say he understood
and he would ever wait.
His devotion was so strong and good.
"Why doubt or hesitate?"

To Paul, Brent was a trusted friend—
now constant at my side—
someone on whom I could depend
and in whom I could confide.
It was usually he who comforted
my Jennie's lonely heart
with assuring words he often said
that he would never part

from her and me and Peter—
as long as he did live,
he would cherish and protect her
with the love he had to give.
Peter did not welcome
Brent's offerings to him.
After Brent's remarks were done,
Peter proudly raised his chin,

and announced," I am the master
of our home with Father gone.
Be careful, Brent, with overtures
where you never could belong."
Brent was shocked and sorrowed.
He tried to understand
that Peter's stance was borrowed
from a vacant father's hand.

With Brent I was less lonely;
he took such special care
of Paul's estate — if only
love were also there!
In the times we spent together,
reluctantly I knew
it was a comfort and a pleasure
to have him close in view.

Chapter Four

One dark day as I was reading
over Paul's estate,
I started crying. I was needing
somehow to relate
the crushing letter sent from Paul
to all the trust and joy
he had brought me all in all
since he was just a boy.

Noticing my tears, Brent tenderly
asked what he could do.
I pled for him to help me see
what was real and true.
He responded that he had to wait
until the time was right
to share some things of Paul's strange fate,
providing new insight.

I sobbed and begged again with grief—
he must tell me then,
and give my heart new-found relief
from fears that would not end.
Brent resisted, then complied.
With a solemn, grave demeanor,
he sat down slowly at my side,
placed his arm around my shoulder.

"Ruth, you know how often Paul and I
took horses on an outing.
Paul was the one to specify
how the ride might be most challenging.
On one of our more distant trips
we traveled to the place
where Paul saw the maiden's smiling lips
and her alluring face—

surrounded by her full black hair;
it shines like new mined coal.
Her form is lithe, and moves with flair
in undulating strolls."
Brent's rapt reflection left me faint.
I reeled with sickening visions.
He tried to keep in his restraint
my rushing, wild derision.

Now Brent could see how sorely
his words had seared my mind.
His tales were handled poorly;
he knew they were unkind.
Yet, he went on explaining
how on that trip with Paul,
Brent had kept complaining,
"Paul! Don't look at her at all!

I warned Paul of her beauty,
and her quest for his attentions.
The warnings were my duty,
though it brought us fierce contention.
As we walked the village square,
she followed close behind.
Paul could not help but stop and stare
whenever he would find

her lingering near him wistfully.
When he asked her name,
she only smiled, knowing he
would surely ask again.
At last she turned and disappeared
within a tavern door.
I held Paul's arm, for it was clear
he wanted to explore

just who she was, and introduce
himself to her as well.
I told him it was just a ruse.
I never could dispel
his persistent thoughts and questions
of who she was, and why
she cast such bold intentions
through her penetrating eyes.

From that time on Paul worried me.
I feared he would return.
One day his curiosity
would send him back to learn
how she had caught his foolish heart,
and would not let it go.
His judgment would be torn apart.
And he would also know

you never could release him
to such a bitter, rank request.
By then, his courage wearing thin,
to not come home was best."
Brent could see I was confounded.
His tears dissolved his pride.
He clenched a fist and pounded
on a table at his side.

"At once I should have told you,
warned you of this threat.
Forevermore this backward view
will fill me with regret."
To Brent it was no staggering surprise
when he learned Paul was gone.
Then the letter gave him rise
to reserve what he had known.

Chapter Five

The days ahead were pleasant,
Jennie's birthday a delight.
Spring is such a grand event.
The warming sun invites
rivulets of melting snow
to meander down the hills
and join the rushing brook below.
I never cease to thrill

with the ending of the winter
as it blusters out the door,
making room for fresh adventures
that springtime can explore.
Then summer glides across each day
with a lazy attitude.
Evenings languish in their winsome way
as they emulate her mood.

Alone within the sanctity
of my private sitting room,
my daydreams wandered peacefully.
The balmy afternoon
led my heart and mind to contemplate
the beauty of the season.
How meadow flowers proliferate!
It was they who gave me reason

to remember and to wonder—
where had Robert gone?
It was early in September.
It seemed so very long
since I had seen him, felt his touch.
His steady, grey-blue eyes
reminded me how very much
they always mystified

my girlhood feelings when we met,
the feelings most of all—
the ones he charmed me to forget,
those I withheld from Paul.
Perhaps the time was near
when old feelings could resume.
A shiver made it clear,
I wished Robert would come soon.

Chapter Six

I was startled with a chilling sense
that someone close behind
was hovering near my head, and hence,
seemed to read my mind!
I vaulted from my wing-back chair,
and turned around to see
that Brent was stiffly standing there
looking down at me.

Without a change of stance—
his voice was crisp and cold—
he announced, with a backward glance,
"Some man has just been told
to wait within the courtyard.
A servant led him there."
He left without another word
and slowly climbed the stairs.

I was stunned at his attitude,
completely unprepared.
"To interrupt my solitude!
How could he have dared?
Announcing guests is not his right;
He a guest as well!
Such an act is impolite."
I felt my anger swell.

I hurried through the entry hall
into the flowered courtyard.
There was Robert standing tall.
It was so very hard
to keep myself from running
into his sheltering arms.
Instead, I stood still, pondering
his never-ending charms.

Robert turned, and when he found
I was waiting to be noticed,
he dropped his gloves upon the ground.
He kept a steady focus
upon my face, my delighted eyes,
and then he spoke my name.
"Ruth, you are a great surprise.
Your beauty is to blame.

My clumsiness on any day
is all because of you.
Whether near to you or far away,
in my mind the view
of your lovely face and form
causes such distraction!"
He made me laugh, as I warned
him of his own attraction.

Flirtatious words—to be sure!
Should I have dared be so playful?
Robert was a welcome cure
for my always being careful
and worried how I acted.
This created such a stress!
It kept my gloom protracted,
and spoiled my happiness.

Robert bent upon his knee
to retrieve his fallen gloves.
Then I saw him look past me
to something up above.
My eyes straightway followed
to an open upper window
where parted curtains had allowed
a darkened form to show.

Brent was standing in the shadows.
Again, he was so rude!
"Does he believe I do not know
his watching has intruded
upon my private visit
with a dear and personal friend?
My social manners are explicit.
His intrusions have to end."

Robert saw I was perplexed.
He asked me what was wrong.
Distraught with what I should do next,
I spoke, "It won't be long
before we have our evening meal.
Please say that you will join us.
New guests to Cook have such appeal;
for them she loves to fuss."

Robert assured me he would stay.
I asked him to remain
in the courtyard while I slipped away
to tell the cook the same.
When I returned, to my pleasure,
Peter had been there.
"Your son is bright and quite mature,"
Robert spoke with care,

to put me readily at ease
without their proper introduction.
(Peter was so very pleased,
to share their conversation
when he and I together
spent some time alone,
and privately we could confer
one day while Brent was gone.)

Peter told me Robert
was so very kind to him.
It seemed he understood the hurt
that Peter held within.
Peter spoke of Paul's long absence.
Robert answered that he knew
his father well; there was a chance
the stories were not true.

"Despite the lack of evidence
to prove the stories wrong,
remember your experiences
with him were very strong.
You knew your father intimately.
Your own memories you should trust.
Carry his name proudly—
not to do so would be unjust."

Robert's words were well received.
Peter was consoled.
As a loyal son he then believed
he could be quite bold
in speaking of his father's name,
and defend him valiantly.
I was amazed such few words came
to set his anger free.

Peter also confided to me
Robert was my only friend
who spoke of Paul so kindly,
and never would offend
our love for him. In a pause,
Peter's words were sent
to let me know that Robert was
a different man than Brent.

Chapter Seven

When dinner had arrived
and we had gathered around the table,
Brent was silent while he eyed
all that he was able
regarding Robert's manners—
especially towards me—
so he could be completely sure
what my response might be.

Brent's behavior was so obvious;
Robert was amused.
I tried to act oblivious.
Soon the children were excused,
as dessert would come much later.
For them it proved the best,
Robert accessed Brent's true nature
by a calculated test:

Robert broke a silence,
by speaking just to Brent
with a pleasant, friendly parlance
to forestall impertinence.
It was clear that Brent was in no mood
to welcome Robert's questions.
Robert, nonetheless, pursued
his queries and suggestions.

"Brent, you must have pressing needs
while managing Paul's estate.
I sympathize, and can proceed
to help alleviate
the pressures. I am quite aware
of expert legal guidance—
attorneys, superb and well prepared
in whom one can have confidence."

Robert then sought to volunteer
a prominent name or two,
trustworthy men he knew for years,
and either one would do.
"Ruth, I will gladly leave the names
for your own attention;
and give them yours just the same,
and definitely mention

how I am very eager they
examine your affairs.
They are competent in every way
to provide the best of care."
Then he turned again to Brent:
"I know you must agree.
I want to see you both content—
it would mean so much to me."

Brent's face began to redden.
He fixed his rival in a stare.
His anger was not hidden
as he leaned back in his chair.
He lifted up his goblet
and slowly sipped his wine.
His long delay—a deliberate threat—
sent a tingle up my spine.

"I have heard enough", he said.
"I know why you are here.
Undoubtedly, now that Paul is dead,
your motives are quite clear.
I well remember who you are.
You met Ruth long ago.
Your business ranges very far;
that I have come to know.

This so-called 'offer' is another means
of gaining Ruth's affection,
so all your shrewd financial schemes
will hinge on that connection.
I manage Ruth, and the property
our family rightly owns.
All her affairs belong to me
as the guardian of her home."

"Now that Paul is dead!" I gasped.
"Why did you say that?"
Brent was flustered, stunned. At last
he jumped from where he sat.
"Just a slip of tongue," he pled.
"You know we both have wondered
if Paul could possibly be dead,
for every search has blundered.

This conversation must dispense.
Robert, you now know
your presence here brings me offense.
I am asking you to go."
Then glowering at me, he left the room.
Who was the one to blame?
Brent's shocking manners had surfaced soon—
right after Robert came.

"Ruth, I know this has troubled you.
Forgive what I have done.
Be patient. Trust that what is true
eventually will come
to end the long bewildering days."
Then Robert cautioned me:
"Be amiable, Ruth, when Brent must stay.
I am sure that he will see

how he has harmed your feelings.
He will regret his burst of temper.
And now I must be leaving.
I will return—perhaps November."
Robert stood, he said no more.
His soberness softened when
I whispered to him at the door,
"Please do come back again."

Chapter Eight

When summertime comes to an end,
the multi-colored leaves—
burnished, bright, resplendent—
excite the autumn breeze
to chase around the meadows
and stir up the dry terrain,
then dance within the shadows
of the tree-lined country lanes.

Smoke from every chimney
drapes a shroud across the sky.
It circles through the dreary,
drifting clouds that mourn and cry
torrential tears of loneliness
for flowers that have gone—
flowers that gentle raindrops blessed
and nourished summer-long.

Winter waits within the wings
of autumn's pageantry,
with an entourage assembling
for its march of majesty.
The barking of the thunder
at the heels of bursting light
awakens every slumbering creature
nestled in the night.

Announcing that the snowflakes
will begin the wintry show,
a whirl-wind bellows, bends and shakes
the trees to let them know
the time has come when leaves prepare
to take their annual rest,
by carpeting the ground they share
with song-birds' fallen nests.

I delighted in the grand parade
of each season's paragon.
The sunshine or the soothing shade
enhances the phenomenon
that nature has invented
with her own creative charms.
Still, I once was more contented
held in Paul's adoring arms.

October was nearing an end,
and Robert had not come.
Brent did all he could to mend
his words he knew had stung
my mind, my heart. The solace
he once had brought to me
diminished when I noticed
I must guard my privacy.

I concealed my troubling questions—
those his outburst piqued
when Robert's bold suggestions
obligated Brent to speak.
"How could Brent say he managed me,
and then go on to claim
that Paul's own family property
belonged to his domain?"

Most of all, when he declared,
"Now that Paul is dead,"
he gave my mind a sudden scare
that lingered in my head.
I let It go, and so did Brent,
never mentioning it again.
The message that his comment sent
he never did explain.

Brent had offered kind relief
on his first trip to my home
to ease my pounding pangs of grief.
I tried to sort alone
every personal detail
which Paul had left behind,
with the hope they would unveil
the mounting mysteries in my mind.

During the two long years that passed,
Brent increased his sojourns,
so he could oversee at last
Paul's business he eagerly learned.
At first I was agreeable.
I had quite enough to do.
It seemed only sensible
to let him keep in view

the relentless business matters
that cluttered up my time.
Paul loved his cousin as a brother.
I had no reason to decline.
Brent's interest kept escalating,
his influence had no end.
His advice became discomforting—
that I should condescend

and request a fair divorcement bill
to set my status free.
He importuned,"A married woman will
never come to be
happy in a circumstance
that holds her future bound
to a missing husband, with little chance
he ever will be found."

Brent's persuasions only made me
ever more resigned.
Though my life was hurt and empty,
lovely memories combined
within a heart that still loved Paul.
No matter how I tried
to forget his voice, his face, and all
the ways he took such pride

in Peter and in Jennie.
They still belonged to him!
Both of them reminded me
how sweet our lives had been—
so full of joy by Paul's warm touch.
For us he deeply cared.
He loved our family home so much
and everything we shared.

No, Brent could never change my mind,
however often, however long
he pressured me to leave behind
the memories that belonged
to no one else but Paul and me.
Brent had no right to claim
that jurisdiction. He could see
his persuasions were in vain.

Chapter Nine

Autumn changed to wintertime,
a time again for Brent to leave,
and return to his estate to sign
some papers he received.
As he had been with me so long,
I welcomed his departure.
And yet, whenever he was gone
I felt more like a dowager.

It was not a pleasant imagery.
Still, my time was nicely spent
with personal domesticity
I could not do while Brent
was watching my occupations.
Until then, I complied
with Robert's admonitions,
letting Brent help me decide

.

how I should manage this or that.
He was pleased to be consulted.
I behaved the perfect diplomat—
easing tensions that resulted
when Robert came and I was vexed
with Brent's rank jealousy.
Notwithstanding how distressed
I had come to be.

It was not fair to disallow
all the good that Brent had done:
his nurturing of Jennie, and how
he was the perfect one
to console her in her father's loss.
His love for her was true.
He would watch over her at any cost.
She loved him dearly, too.

Peter felt quite differently;
he remained aloof from Brent.
Paul and I had tried to see
what such a young boy's actions meant.
As Brent and Paul were cousins,
the family ties were strong.
Why would Paul's own son
prefer that Brent did not belong?

Peter's rancor escalated
through the dark and dismal days,
while news of Paul awaited.
He resented Brent's delays—
remaining on our premise
to see our business done.
Peter made a solemn promise:
"I shall be the one

who manages our own estate,
as stipulated in the will.
I also know that I must wait
most patiently until
I become of legal age
to accept my father's charge.
Then I will swiftly disengage
Brent, and set at large

his time and his intentions
to the ventures of his own.
Then he will need my invitation
to come into our home."
I sympathized with Peter.
In his father's grievous absence
he was meant to be a leader,
and sought out every chance.

Chapter Ten

Brent was gone for several weeks;
December drawing near.
In time, he would return to keep
the promise he made clear,
that our Christmas would be up to him.
He planned a celebration—
the best that there had ever been—
widely sending invitations

to gather all our many friends
for a gala Christmas ball.
Festivities in my home would end
the loneliness of all
the waiting and the wondering
that held me in seclusion.
My troubled heart began to sing
with sweet anticipation.

One day as I was wandering
by an upstairs bedroom window,
a most peculiar, sudden feeling
prompted me to follow
closer to the frosty pane.
I strained my eyes to look
toward the covered bridge that stretched
across the frozen brook.

It bordered on our property,
some distance from our manor.
Moments passed. Then I could see
hooves, in such a clamor,
pounding through the snowdrifts.
Four horses pulled a coach.
Stunned, I stood there marveling if
someone dared approach

our private courtyard entry
without a proper introduction.
No gentleman would ever be
bereft of that instruction.
The coach eased up slowly
as the horses came to rest.
I focused my anxious eyes to see
the uninvited guest.

From the darkness of the coach floor
stepped the figure of a man.
The coachman held the open door
where I saw another's hand
reaching for assistance.
Was he old or was he hurt?
Even from that distance
I could see that it was Robert

standing in the snow,
offering up his gentle arms
to buoy a man I did not know .
It filled me with alarm.
"Why would Robert ever want
to bring a stranger here,
especially one not ambulant—
and at this time of year?"

I rushed downstairs to see them,
though staying out of view.
The servants flocked to help them when
they saw someone they knew
who had been invited previously.
Of course, Robert was a friend!
No one yet had noticed me—
that which I did intend.

Leaning heavily on Robert's shoulder,
the other man could barely say,
"Thank you, my dear friend. For surely
I cannot repay
all that you have done for me."
When they reached the entry hall,
I felt the shock. "Could it be?
Dear God, he looks like Paul!"

Chapter Eleven

I awakened from a whirling faint
with Robert sitting at my side.
I badly needed his restraint,
for I panicked and I cried.
I tried to rise from where I lay;
Robert firmly held my hands—
imploring me to stay
so he could help me understand

what had happened to me,
and what was taking place.
I had awakened, desperately
searching Robert's face
to see if he was really there.
My confusion was extreme.
I wondered if the whole affair
was just a dreadful dream.

"Who was that man? Where did he go?"
My voice was choked with fear.
I trembled as I spoke, and so
Robert held me near.
"Was it Paul I saw with you?
Please, I do not want to see him!
Where is that maiden?" Robert knew
my rambling was without reason

"Ruth, I know this is great surprise.
For now, forget about that maiden.
Paul has been sorely victimized;
    the abuse was heavy laden."
As Robert softly spoke to me,
    I listened with intent.
He shared a shocking story,
    after gaining my consent

to tell of his own involvement
    in the quest for finding Paul.
Robert proved a powerful instrument,
    more capable than all
the countless people I engaged
    to do investigations.
Robert's rare connections staged
    astute re-explorations.

He told me from the moment
that he first learned Paul was missing—
and heard the ugly rumors foment
through the widespread talebearing—
he was sure the stories all ensued
    from calculated lies.
For Paul could never be untrue;
    he would never womanize.

Robert knew Paul loved me—
more than his own life.
He knew whatever came to be,
Paul was loyal to his wife.
Without my ever knowing,
nor any of my friends,
Robert had been unwavering
in pursuing to the end

to find wherever Paul might be.
And if he were alive,
he would bring him safely home to me.
When they both arrived,
the shock was much too great to bear;
the stories, still too vivid.
The dark, distressing long affair
I started to relive.

Robert sent the manservants
to put Paul into bed.
His instructions, clear and fervent;
they did everything he said.
He told me Paul was very ill,
and must have a doctor's care.
He should stay in bed until
the one he called was there

to monitor the patient's progress
and guide him back to health.
Paul had suffered great distress—
he must explain himself.
"I will only tell you where
he recently has been.
I was led to a foreign land. There
I found him in a prison.

Arrested as a vagrant,
with no money and no way
to prove any of his statements,
Paul was forced to stay.
When I arrived, the prison guards
were willing to comply
with my proposed rewards—
large sums of money that would buy

Paul's immediate release
into my custody.
Their greed was readily increased.
Not one would disagree.
Our travel home was long;
the ocean voyage rough.
Yet, Paul's resolve was strong,
and always just enough

to let him make the journey.
All he thought about was you,
and Peter, and his Jennie.
It helped him make it through
every measured moment,
every hard-earned step.
Due to what he underwent,
many nights he hardly slept.

Ruth, it is time for me to go.
There is nothing you should fear.
I am sure that by tomorrow
the doctor will be here.
I now have urgent business
that requires my journey home.
I also feel it will be best
you and Paul are left alone.

Before Brent comes, Paul needs to share
all his misadventures—
just with you—and have your care
through all he must endure.
There is a confrontation yet
that needs to be completed,
before Paul ever can forget
the way he has been treated."

I was still quite shaken,
urging Robert not to leave.
"Abandoned and forsaken!
What else must I believe?"
I would help Paul get better.
Somehow I would adjust.
But there was still the letter
which had shattered all my trust.

Trudging silently and slowly
to Robert's carriage door,
reluctantly, I did agree
to let him go before
the weather could grow worse;
dark clouds were hanging low.
By night his coach could not traverse
the ever-deepening snow.

Tears were dripping from my eyes.
Both my head and heart were aching.
"Robert, don't you realize
you seem to be forsaking
what we both again were feeling?
And, yet, you brought Paul home!"
Such thoughts I kept concealing—
they were meant for me alone.

Robert stood beside me;
his grey-blue eyes surveyed my face.
Surely he could clearly see
I longed for his embrace.
With his manly understanding,
he kept a formal distance.
His inmost affections building,
we both needed his resistance.

Somehow amid my blinding tears,
I began to speak:
"Despite how long the future years,
forever I will keep
remembering all your kind advice;
and truly most of all
the unselfish, noble sacrifice
that you have made for Paul."

Robert caught the deeper meaning
of my endearing exclamation.
He complicated all my feelings
by his own clear declaration:
"Ruth, I never will forget you,
in the future or from the past."
He climbed into his coach, and through
a signal that he cast,

the coachman snapped the horses' reins.
They gave a stinging crack.
The horses, suddenly unconstrained,
started lurching back,
until the coachman's skillful voice
guided them on a forward lunge.
By then I had no other choice
but to watch that scene expunge

Robert from my lingering gaze.
The coach wheels' rolling sound
echoed through the heavy haze
that lay upon the ground.
I stood stiffly in the snow. Somehow,
I heard a voice that said,
"Ma'am, your husband has been sleeping—now
we think he may be dead."

Chapter Twelve

The next few nights were dark and frightening.
Paul had lapsed into a coma.
Each dreary day following,
the doctor brought another formula
meant to strengthen Paul's weak frame,
as soon as he could start
to eat or drink. I fought the pain
that swelled within my heart.

Sitting at Paul's bedside,
I perused his weary face.
Sympathy erased my pride,
and all my doubts were chased
away with every memory
that could withhold my love from Paul.
Robert's warning came back to me.
"What 'confrontation' must befall

our long-delayed reunion
whenever Paul has gained his strength?
How I need Paul's full communion
to know what Robert meant!"
I yearned for my husband's recovery,
to hold him in my arms.
I begged in prayers he soon would be
restored from every harm

that had beset his failing body,
and now confined his brilliant mind
in this—another prison. Would he
again leave me behind
to mourn for him anew?
How could I then console the children?
They would not believe it could true
their father's weakening condition

might not be healed. They promised me
that he would fully recover.
Peter's hopes were strong as steel.
Jennie nursed me as a mother,
bringing me my meals,
wrapping shawls around my shoulders.
For the wintry sun was long concealed,
and the nights were getting colder.

The doctor on one fateful day
approached me privately.
"Ruth, this is hard for me to say,
but I cannot let this be
delayed a moment longer,
and permit false expectations.
Your husband won't recover;
you must make your preparations."

At midnight, in my exhaustive sleep,
I saw Paul in a dream—
strong and well, his frame complete.
His handsome features gleamed,
and brought a flood of memories.
He seemed so full of joy.
His countenance reminded me
of when he was a boy,

and all the playful times we shared—
how quickly they appeared!
They happily scampered, unimpaired,
within the atmosphere
that hung so darkly in my mind.
They demanded sweet release
of all my anger. My heart enshrined
Paul's love, and brought me peace.

Twelve solemn, steady measured chimes
strode across my reveries.
A clock was sounding out the time
to rise up from my knees.
My weary arms and aching head
were resting where I lay
upon the quilt across Paul's bed
where I had knelt to pray.

I peered into the darkened room.
A candle flickered peacefully.
The moonlight from the window illumined
what I then would see.
Cast upon the adjoining wall,
a shadow, clear and plain,
was rising, swaying; then seemed to fall,
and then it rose again.

I watched its undulations—
which almost lulled me back to sleep—
then I felt a strange sensation.
I heard someone softly speak.
At that moment I discerned the shadow
was a human arm and hand.
Alarmed, I pushed upon my elbows,
about to rise and stand.

When I looked across the bed,
I saw Paul's hand raised in the air,
swaying weakly above his head
to signal someone he was there.
He was fully wide awake!
I began to cry.
My sobbing made my body shake.
The doctor standing by

bent to examine Paul's gray face;
and with a smile upon his own,
he took Paul's hand in a strong embrace.
Not leaving me alone—
his other hand upon my shoulder—
he tenderly spoke my name.
"Ruth, a miracle has just occurred.
You have your husband back again."

Chapter Thirteen

The days ahead were joyous.
Paul's recovery swift and strong.
Our Nanny, cook and servants fussed
to help the task along.
In my private, quiet moments,
I continued in my prayers
of thankfulness for the grace God sent
that Paul was with me there.

Embraced by loving children
who were ever at his side,
they cheered his heart, and always won
his laughter when they tried
to beat him at their parlor games,
or tell a funny story.
They lifted his residual pains
and convinced him not to worry.

What lay ahead was yet to be
a challenge of great proportions.
Paul needed full recovery
to control his fierce emotions.
They wrenched his long-tormented mind
and engulfed his battered body.
When his haunting memories then combined,
they always frightened me.

He embraced my love so gratefully
before he told his dreadful news.
I had forgiven him completely
for all the stories I thought were true.
When he was well enough to speak
at length and bear my shock
of what he must reveal, and seek
the strength to fully talk

of every sordid detail, from
the start until the end,
he shared the cruel betrayal of one
he loved and called his friend.
It was true about the maiden
with the wide and wandering eyes,
who had flirted with the village men.
So they were not surprised

when Paul hoisted her upon his horse
and they galloped away with speed.
Since no one knew their intended course,
the village men had all agreed
their disappearance simply meant
they had run away together.
They assured each official sent
as an interrogator.

The maiden did engage Paul's eye
in the village square.
Yet, she told a calculated lie:
Brent was in danger there
at the outskirts of the village.
He had sent her stealthily,
knowing Paul would have the courage
to come and set him free.

Without the slightest hesitation—
for Paul was most alarmed;
he trusted her presentation—
convinced, not by her charms,
but by the fact she knew Brent's name,
and he would know that Paul was there.
For Brent was visiting at their aunt's domain
while Paul, with studious care,

attended to her grand estate.
When Paul would leave for home,
Brent knew the route he would take,
and the large and lovely roan
Paul had selected for his requisite ride.
The maiden did readily see—
both were clearly and well described—
recognizing Paul was easy.

She lured Paul to a den of thieves.
Brent was also there.
But he was perfectly at ease
without a single care,
except to mock Paul viciously:
"Oh, Paul, you foolish man—
seduced to impropriety
by such a clever plan!

You have a lovely, trusting wife
awaiting your return.
How mean of you to upset her life,
when she has to learn
that you have now forsaken her
for a ravishing maiden's charms.
So I will be her comforter
and hold her in my arms.

Dear Paul, how I have hated you
and your every great advantage!
I prepared this rendezvous
these men helped me to manage.
I have worked with them before.
They will handsomely be paid
with money that I have in store.
So you need not be afraid

that your estate will pay this bill.
Yet, you have to know, in time,
all your money, wife and children will
eventually be mine.
And now, dear cousin, you must agree
to pen the perfect letter
to your wife, so she will see
that you love another better,

possessing such beauty and allure,
she simply took you for the asking.
And what is more, your love for her
is passionate and everlasting.
If you refuse to write the letter,
I will have no other choice
than to kidnap little Peter.
But, by then I will have no voice

as to what these friends of mine might do,
even with a ransom.
Peter may end up like you—
a slave. Must your son
be placed in abject misery
because you did not care
enough to let him remain free?
Think of his mother waiting there,

crying over his disappearance.
Her grief will be much greater
than hers for you—don't take the chance.
Your decision cannot come later."
Paul was trapped; he did comply.
His own fate had now begun.
He was taken to a ship to die,
shanghaied to sail the ocean.

The brutal boatswain took each turn
to lash Paul without mercy.
The prisoner had everything to learn
as he worked the rugged sea.
For a year the captain held him bound.
He never walked on land,
until one day Paul finally found
an escape the sailors planned.

Every one of them succeeded,
except the most infirm.
Paul got away unheeded.
He held a great concern
for the youngest of the sailors—
who was just a lad.
He reminded Paul of Peter,
which often made him sad

to see someone that young
be abused and so forsaken.
Paul helped the boy along
(which brought more risks than need be taken).
Eventually, Paul was seen and caught
just after he procured
a place of comfort where he thought
the lad would be secure.

Paul was ordered to the prison
nearly two more years - until
Robert valiantly had found him,
destitute and ill.
All the stories Brent had told me
were extensions of the lies
he had started. For Paul and he
had never on their rides

seen the maiden with black hair,
nor spent any time at all
wandering in that village square
where Brent said she followed Paul.
Now the time had come when Brent
unknowingly would arrive
to face his cousin whom he had sent
to death—yet still alive.

Chapter Fourteen

This time Paul knew exactly how
to answer Brent's derision.
The future for them both would now
be entirely Paul's decision.
For he was prepared by every means
to counter Brent's disputes,
should he deny his wicked schemes
in an effort to refute

the accusations Paul would make.
Brent's cunning protestations
would prove to be a grand mistake;
he would have no vindication.
Paul's tall and sturdy stature, strong
and formidable alone,
stood well what he endured the long
two years away from home.

Memories filled him with a greater strength
than his weakened body drew
to face the challenge. And at length,
whatever Brent might do
would be of little consequence
compared to Paul's resolve
to end his long ordeal, and hence,
every mystery would be solved.

Brent sent a fond note to me
that foretold of his arrival.
Paul's presence would immediately be
a shock most confrontational.
Brent's conduct could turn quite ugly.
Paul wanted me away
from the sordid possibility
that Brent might soon display

violent words or actions
which I must not hear or see.
The children's aggrieved reactions
must be spared. I did agree
to have them leave. I presumed
the servants would be near.
I would remain in an adjoining room,
so I could see and hear

everything that would be done—
Brent unaware I was listening.
As the children would be gone,
he would assume I was with them.
Brent arrived as we expected.
The day was grey and bitter cold.
The servants were directed
to only say what they were told.

Brent went straightway to the fireplace,
and stood facing toward the flames
to warm his hands. His leering face
spoke of how he came
again to take complete control
of Paul's estate and family.
Pondering that cunning, evil goal,
Brent slowly turned around to see

Paul sitting in the wing-back chair
not far from where Brent stood.
Paul spoke with an unwavering stare,
"I know that this is rude
to not have given you a party
to celebrate your return.
But then, you surely must agree,
I have a lot to learn

about how to greet a cousin—
one I counted as a friend.
Perhaps you can be of help therein;
what would you recommend?"
Brent was more than silent.
He seemed not even to breathe.
Standing rigid, he made no attempt
to find a way to leave.

The cousins began exchanging
sharp daggers with their eyes.
Brent's internal hate was raging.
Paul could not disguise
his fierce resolve to make Brent pay
for his cruelty and deceit.
Brent launched his smoldering role-play,
and poised himself to speak:

"This is not a great surprise.
I have pondered what to do
if you came home to tell your lies
of just what happened to you.
You have no proof to absolve your blame,
which witnesses have affirmed.
Everything they have to claim
your own letter has confirmed.

And what about sweet Ruth
and all the torment which you have brought,
when at last she knew the truth
about that gypsy-wench you sought?
No, Paul, you are not threatening,
just because you have survived
the consequences of your sins,
and by chance you are still alive.

And so, dear Paul, I will resign you now
to all your fantasies."
He gave his cousin a pretentious bow
and smugly turned to leave.
Paul rose up swiftly, straight and tall,
and seized Brent by his shoulders,
and shoved him hard against the wall;
his resolve growing bolder.

As he held Brent firmly in his grip,
Paul confronted him face to face:
"Your traitorous, sneering, lying lips
will never again disgrace
my home, my name, my family,
and most of all my wife!
Your malevolent, scheming hypocrisy
will cost the freedom of your life.

Now get out of here, you serpent, before
I cannot control my rage."
Paul threw his cousin on the floor.
Brent, in his own rampage,
leaped upon his feet and stormed
into the entry hall.
"This you will regret," he warned,
"Ruth trusts me most of all.

She will not accept your tales
of thieves and sailing ships!"
Suddenly Brent's face went pale,
as he heard what crossed his lips.
"Sailing ships?" I spoke, from where
I stood nearby the entry.
Brent reeled in shock; he was now aware
that I could plainly see

his performance from the start
of his coming to our home.
He snatched up his coat and darted
through our entry door alone.
I glanced at Paul and cried,
"How can you let Brent get away?"
"My dear Ruth," Paul replied,
"soon this very day

he will be apprehended
by authorities who wait
where our property is extended,
beyond the arbor gate.
Come sit down beside me, Ruth,
there is more for me to share.
Robert is an amazing sleuth.
He not only found me where

I served a prison sentence,
and restored me to my home.
He also found the evidence
to incriminate Brent alone
for his treachery against me,
and his plot to have me dead.
Robert found the captain by the sea
on the dock where I was led.

The captain was willing to admit
his cohorts had been paid
by some gentleman who was very rich.
And part of what they made
they offered him if he would deport
this vagabond on his ship.
He readily complied, for he was short
of men to make the trip.

I vehemently protested,
and offered the captain more
of my own money, if unmolested
I remained upon the shore.
With reason he thought I lied,
just as other men had done.
He took me, securely tied,
to the ship's ruthless boatswain.

A court will hear the testimonies
of the captain and the maiden
who recounted her false story
that led me to Brent's den.
Her beauty is so stunning,
her identity so clear.
She was willing to stop running,
and take the chance to swear

the truth about Brent's devious plot.
For he had also lied
with his promises to her that bought
her eagerness to guide
me to that vile, dark den of thieves,
where Brent had set his trap.
He promised her if she would leave
and never would come back,

he would arrange to send her money
regularly for her keep.
She had no choice but to agree,
and promise not to speak
of what she knew of villainous Brent.
He threatened her as well.
She knew just what his warnings meant.
and vowed to never tell."

Chapter Fifteen

The trial was held; Paul testified.
The captain and the maiden
convinced the jury how Brent had lied,
and brutalized his cousin.
The thieves had up and disappeared.
(To the court they were not needed.)
Three separate witnesses had appeared;
their veracity was heeded.

Brent promptly was incarcerated.
He now lives a broken man.
And Paul, still broken hearted,
travels when he can
to the prison with the quest
to reconcile with Brent,
and offer his forgiveness—
still cherishing the sentiments,

remembering the good times
and their countless mutual joys.
In the days before Brent's change of mind,
they were beloved friends as boys.
Brent will not comply;
he refuses Paul's petition.
Paul will ever try,
hoping Brent will one day listen.

Brent will never be informed
of a thoughtful, generous plan.
Before his wicked scheme was born
and his betrayal of Paul began,
Paul was making preparations
for his cousin to equally share
their aunt's estate. It was being done
with privacy and care.

Robert sold his property,
became a prominent statesman.
Busy with his duties, he
has never come again
for a visit with us in our home.
We have written our proceedings
to let him know the task is done,
ending Brent's blackhearted dealings.

Occasional news informs us well
where Robert's service grows.
Our gratitude for him still swells,
we try to let him know.
He remains preoccupied
and mostly out of view.
A wife and child are at his side,
his letters now are few.

Throughout our country manor,
our children's voices sing.
We make a joyous clamor,
when early in the spring
we romp out in the meadow
and stroll the village square.
My happiness in constant glow—
Paul again is with me there.

Georgia Jensen Blosil began joyfully composing tunes on the piano and writing imaginary stories when just a very little girl. Before she could understand and utilize a dictionary, she would ask her patient mother to spell words for her. Her love of creative writing has deepened and continued throughout her life.

She is a graduate of the University of California at Berkeley where she studied music. Her music compositions have been performed by choirs and instrumentalists in many programs and concerts. In recent years, Georgia has enjoyed not only writing music, but also poetry, and stories in verse for children.

She and her husband, Warren, are the parents of six sons and a daughter, and presently have twenty-one grandchildren. Her family is her constant source of purpose, inspiration, and joy.

Her other literary publications include the books: *"Where Was Mary"* ; *"Divine Reflections" A Poetic Trilogy* ; and the poems, *"Little Hands."*